D1519300

Tales
of Adam

Tales
of Adam

DANIEL QUINN

Illustrated by Michael McCurdy

STEERFORTH PRESS
HANOVER, NEW HAMPSHIRE

For information about permission to reproduce
selections from this book, write to:
Steerforth Press L.C., 25 Lebanon Street
Hanover, New Hampshire 03755

Library of Congress Cataloging-in-Publication Data

Quinn, Daniel.
Tales of Adam / Daniel Quinn.
p. cm.
ISBN 1-58642-074-7 (hardcover : alk. paper)
1. Adam (Biblical figure) — Fiction. 2. Abel (Biblical figure) —
Fiction. 3. Bible. O.T. — History of Biblical events — Fiction.
4. Nature — Effect of human beings on — Fiction.
5. Hunting and gathering societies — Fiction.
6. Prehistoric peoples — Fiction.
7. Fathers and sons — Fiction. I. Title.

PS3567.U338T35 2005
813'.54–DC21

2003009152

ISBN-13 978-1-58642-074-1

FIRST EDITION

INTRODUCTION

*I*shmael, the work for which I am best known, is a literary curiosity, being the eighth version of a book I labored on for some thirteen years. In each version I followed a slightly different path and made slightly different discoveries.

Some of these discoveries could be carried forward from one version to the next, and some—equally valuable or even more valuable—had to be left behind. The tales in this volume fall into this latter category. They were originally part of the fourth version, called *The Book of Nahash* (*nahash* being the Hebrew word for "serpent"). While the book as a whole didn't accomplish what I wanted it to accomplish (that was a thing that didn't happen until *Ishmael*), these tales have a life of their own that seems to me worth preserving.

DANIEL QUINN

THE SIGN OF
ABUNDANCE

When the gods set out to make the universe, they said to themselves, "Let us make of it a manifestation of our unending abundance and a sign to be read by those who shall have eyes to read. Let us lavish care without stint on every thing: no less upon the most fragile blade of grass than upon the mightiest of stars, no less upon the gnat that sings for an hour than upon the mountain that stands for a millennium, no less upon a flake of mica than upon a river of gold. Let us make no two leaves the same from one branch to the next, no two branches the same from one tree to the next, no two trees the same from one land to the next, no two lands the same from one world to the next, no two worlds the same from one star to the next. In this way, the Law of Life will be plain to all who shall have eyes to read: the rabbit that creeps out to feed, the fox that lies in wait, the eagle that circles above, and the man who bends his bow to the sky."

And this was how it was done from first to last, no two things alike in all the mighty universe, no single thing made with less care than any other thing throughout generations of

species more numerous than the stars. And those who had eyes to see read the sign and followed the Law of Life.

THE
BUSINESS OF
A RABBIT

God is life in abundance wherever life is found, but not for all in every season. When the locusts thrive, the birds feast and the bison and the deer go hungry; still that place is as full of life as it was before and as full of life as it can be. No place where there is life is a desert, except to man.

It happened once that Adam was camped in such a place and had spent the day in luckless hunting. When he saw it was time to turn back, he said to his son Abel, "Tonight must be our night to go hungry; the god has nothing for us." But just then a young goat crossed their path and Adam slew it. Lifting it to his shoulder, Adam said, "Come, let's hurry back to camp and make a feast of it with your mother."

But as they were crossing a stream near sunset, Abel saw a rabbit at the water's edge and quickly raised his throwing stick. Before he could let fly, however, Adam put a hand over his son's hand and held it fast in the air.

"Don't you see it, Father?" Abel cried. "There's a rabbit drinking at the stream!"

"I see it," Adam replied.

"Then why did you stop me? It's run away now. I might have killed it!"

Adam (who was only now beginning to prepare Abel for the hunter's life) would soon become more experienced as a teacher, but for the moment he was caught flat-footed and could think of no way to answer his son's objection. At last he mumbled a reply that seemed to him far from satisfactory, though it was the best he could do: "That rabbit had some business of its own to finish."

Abel, as yet just a child, was full of questions about this, asking what business the rabbit might have had to finish and how his father had known of it, leaving Adam feeling foolish and inadequate, because of course he hadn't the slightest idea what business the rabbit might have had to finish; this was just a manner of speaking, but he didn't know how to explain that to Abel. That night in camp, after the goat had been butchered and eaten, Adam saw that his son was still puzzling over the rabbit, so he thought for a while and finally said to him: "Here's a story for you. One day my son Abel went out hunting by himself and his path crossed the path of a lion returning to its den. This lion had been hunting all day without luck and knew that its mate and cubs would be hungry. So it fell upon Abel, killed him, and carried him off to its den. Now tell me what you think of this story and what I would do if this happened to you in fact."

Abel thought for a while and said, "I think you would grieve for me."

"You're right," Adam replied. "I would grieve for you, but I wouldn't be angry with the lion for taking what the god had sent for its hunger. Now here's a second story. One day Abel went

out hunting by himself and his path crossed the path of a lion returning to its den. This lion was carrying a goat in its jaws, but seeing Abel it dropped the goat and fell upon him, saying to itself, 'I will have the goat and the boy as well.' Now tell me what you think of this story and what I would do if this happened to you in fact."

Abel thought again and said, "I think no lion would do that."

"You're wrong," Adam replied. "A certain kind of lion would do that, and I would track it down and kill it, because it's a lion gone mad, a lion that kills whatever it sees, beyond need. It's thinking: 'If I kill everything I see, then the gods will have no power over me and will never be able to say, "Today it's the lion's turn to go hungry, today it's the lion's turn to starve, today it's the lion's turn to die." I'll kill everything in the world so that I alone may live. I'll eat the hare that would have been the fox's, and the fox will die; I'll eat the antelope that would have been the wolf's and the wolf will die; but I will live. I shall decide who eats and who starves, who lives and who dies. In this way I shall live forever and thwart the gods.' And this madness makes the lion into a murderer of all life."

Then Adam went on: "The goat and the rabbit we saw today both belonged to the life of this place, which is god; both were living in its hand, as were we. But the rabbit was not ours to kill. The goat was ours; the god sent it to us as its gift. But the rabbit still belonged to the god; it had another hour or another day or another year to live in the god's hand. To have killed it would have been to steal what belonged to the god, and that would have been murder."

The next day was another luckless day of hunting for Adam and his son, and near sunset they turned toward their camp empty-handed. But as they crossed the stream they found the same rabbit waiting at the water's edge. Adam slew it and said to Abel: "You see now that there was no need for us to snatch this rabbit from the hand of the god to save against tomorrow, for the god meant to give it to us anyway: if not the rabbit, some other creature. The god meant the rabbit to live another day, as now, by sending us this rabbit, it means us to live another day. The fire of life burns forever because god gives one to another without stint, each in its own time."

So it was that, in those days, the gods were allowed to tend the garden they had sown. Where they sent the fire of life, there it flowed, and where they turned it aside, there it ebbed, as they would have it. And as they had written in the universe as a whole, so they wrote on earth: that no two things would be made alike in the same generation or from one generation to the next. They wrote this in the very scheme of things, so that every kind and every species grew and changed in their hands, generation after generation, age after age.

And the kind called Man or Adam or Homo grew and changed no less than the rest under the Law of Life, so that over tens of thousands of centuries Homo habilis became Homo erectus, and Homo erectus became Homo sapiens. But all were of the human kind and all were hunter-gatherers generation after generation without exception, and as such were followers of the same Law and the same life as the sparrow and the bear and the dolphin.

And through these hundreds of thousands of

generations of them, the gods found no cause to rebuke them for their lives or to give them statutes for their governance or to send them teachers for their enlightenment or to raise up prophets for their salvation, for they were already following the single Law they had written in the universe for all to follow and so were living in their hands.

TRACKS

One day Adam took his son Abel into the forest. The birds were making a racket in the trees above, and Adam stopped in the path and signaled to his son to do the same. For a while, neither of them moved or spoke; then

Abel said, "Why are we stopping here, Father?" But Adam signaled with his hand: Be still.

Soon the forest grew quiet and Adam said softly: "The birds have forgotten we're here and have stopped giving the alarm. Be still and watch." And as Adam and Abel watched, the creatures of the forest that had hidden during the alarm of the birds reappeared one by one to resume their interrupted activities. The mouse, the mole, the badger, the raccoon, the squirrel, and the deer all went about their business as though Adam and Abel were invisible. As each moved, Adam showed Abel its track and how every pause to feed, every hesitation to reconnoiter, every momentary fright or hurried step could be read plainly in the path. Adam then held out his open hand, and, without understanding why he was to do so, Abel studied the tracks to be found there in his father's palm.

Finally Adam led his son back along the path by which they had entered the forest, pointing out where their tracks had been crossed or followed by other creatures going about their business. When at last they left the forest and Adam said nothing more, Abel asked his father to explain the meaning of what he'd been shown. "There's nothing to explain," Adam replied. "Every track begins and ends in the hand of god. Every track is a lifetime long."

But Abel wasn't satisfied with this answer and asked his father to go on. Adam thought for a while and said, "Hunter and hunted are both standing in their tracks when they meet, and there are no tracks, however far-flung, that fall outside the hand of god."

But Abel continued to press his father with questions. At last Adam said, "All paths lie together in the hand of god like a web endlessly woven, and yours and mine are no greater or less than the beetle's or the squirrel's or the sparrow's. All are held together."

And beyond this Adam could think of nothing more to say.

THE
COCKROACH
WHO HELD A
MOUNTAIN
ON HIS BACK

*L*ate one fall Adam and his family prepared to move their camp, which was made in the place under the little hills. Abel was still a boy at this time and he asked: "Why are we leaving?"

Adam replied: "Do you remember how it was when we came to this place in the summer? The game was plentiful, and berries, grain, fruit, and nuts grew everywhere. But now the game has fled beyond our reach, and the trees and fields nearby have given us their bounty. You've seen that finding what we need takes us farther from camp every day. To stay longer would only exhaust us to no purpose."

Abel asked if they would return the following year. Adam said, "No, not next year, nor the next, but in the third year we'll return."

Adam then led his son far up into the hills one last time, and Abel asked: "Why are we hunting, Father? There's food in our camp for today." Adam smiled and replied, "If the god sends us

something, we'll take it, not for our convenience but for our need. The journey to our winter camp is a long one and we'll have little time for hunting."

As they walked up into the hills, it began to snow heavily, and Abel said, "Let's turn back, Father, or we'll freeze to death here." But Adam said, "We won't freeze to death," and pressed on.

Before long they found fresh tracks in the snow, and Adam said, "Come, I'll show you how to outrun a hare, then you'll be warm." As they followed the trail, Adam explained what Abel was to do in the chase, and soon they came in sight of their quarry.

Having heard the hunters approach, the hare was crouching motionless in the snow, where it was almost invisible. But when the hunters still came on and were only a few paces away, the hare sprang up and bolted forward. The hunters gave chase but were quickly outdistanced until Adam shouted, "Now!" and veered to the left. Following his father's instructions, Abel veered to the right, but saying to himself, "We'll never outrun this hare!" At the same moment, however, the hare turned right, directly into Abel's path, and the boy easily scooped it up on the run.

Astonished, Abel asked his father how he'd known when the hare was going to turn aside in this way. "When you're chasing a hare, watch its ears," Adam replied. "Just before it turns, it will lay them back along its neck. This is your signal to veer to one side or the other. If you guess right, the hare will run straight into your hands. If you guess wrong and it runs the other way, you only have to stalk it again and hope that your second guess is better."

As the hunters turned back toward their camp, it was snowing even more heavily, and Abel's teeth began to chatter. "Why are you making so much noise?" Adam asked, and his son said he was cold. "Then let's stop and warm up," Adam said and sat down in the snow.

"Aren't you going to build a fire?" Abel asked. But his father said, "Building a fire is one way to be warm. This is another. Sit down quietly and stop thinking of the cold as an enemy bent on your destruction."

Abel did as he was told, but his teeth continued to chatter and he pulled his clothes close around him. Watching him, his father remarked, "It's your clothes that are making you cold." Adam held up the hare they'd caught and said, "It wasn't its fur that kept this hare warm. It and the cold were simply one thing."

Adam then took off all his clothes and set them aside. "That's better," he said. "I'm feeling warmer already." But Abel wouldn't take off his clothes and soon he was shaking like a bird in the jaws of a fox.

"Perhaps listening to a story will warm you up," Adam said. "Let's see if I can think of one." After a while he began.

There once was a young cockroach who lived under a tree on a mountainside (Adam began). He was a very brave and stalwart young cockroach but also very headstrong. As he grew up he learned what it is to be a cockroach, but being headstrong he rejected it. "We cockroaches make way," his father had told him. "We make way for everything, and that's why we survive. At the approach of the slightest danger, we make ourselves as thin as a leaf and slip into the narrowest crack around."

But the young cockroach found this approach to life cowardly and contemptible. "It's true that we can make ourselves as thin as leaves," he said, "but didn't the gods give us a good, tough shell to protect us? I refuse to make way for anything. The place my body occupies is mine. I will not abandon it by making myself as thin as a leaf and scuttling into a crack. I will defend it with my good, tough shell."

One day a leaf from the tree fell on top of him, but he stood his ground, saying to the leaf, "You shall not have this place. I will not abandon it by making myself as thin as you and scuttling into a crack. I will not make way for you." And the cockroach withstood the leaf and before long it blew away.

Soon a nut from the tree fell on top of him, but the cockroach stood his ground, saying to the nut, "I know that if I made myself as thin as

a leaf, you would come to rest in the place my body now occupies, but this is my place and you shall not have it. I will not make way for you." And he withstood the nut and soon it rolled away.

But before long a heavy stone came tumbling down the mountainside and landed right on top of the cockroach. All the same, the cockroach stood his ground, saying to the rock, "I know that of all the places on earth you have picked the one encompassed by my body as your resting place for the centuries to come, but you shall not have it. I will not yield it to you by making myself as thin as a leaf. I will not make way for you." And, his legs trembling with exertion and his back aching, the cockroach withstood the stone and soon it toppled off his shell and rolled away.

But the stone had only been the beginning of

an avalanche, for it was time for this mountain to collapse. Soon the whole thing fell over right onto the cockroach. Yet even under this enormous weight, the cockroach held his ground, saying, "You think that just because you're a mountain you can make me give way, but I won't. You may overwhelm the rest of the world—all the seas and valleys and plains of it—but I will deny to you this tiny space my body encompasses. I will not abandon it by making myself as thin as a leaf."

And for a brief moment, his legs wobbling and all his muscles shaking with exertion, this foolhardy cockroach held the entire weight of the mountain on his back. Then, of course, he collapsed and was instantly squashed as thin as a leaf.

Abel, still shivering uncontrollably, stared at his father dumbly, and at last Adam went on.

"You're shaking just the way the cockroach was shaking under the weight of the mountain. Your muscles are protesting the hopeless task you've given them, the task of denying to the cold the tiny space your body encompasses. It can't be done, and your muscles know it. If you don't make way, you will be crushed. In either case, the cold will have the space you're trying to defend. It has already entered into everything in these hills—into the ground, into the trees, into the birds and animals and insects, even into me. You alone are suffering because you alone are trying to push back this mighty force with the strength of your puny muscles.

"The mountain wasn't his enemy, but the cockroach made it into one and so was crushed. The cold isn't your enemy either but it will crush you as though it were an enemy if you don't make way."

"I don't know how," Abel chattered.

"Relax your muscles," his father replied. "Stop struggling to keep the cold out. Let it flow through your body. Give it the space it will have in any case. Then you'll see that it isn't malevolent or hostile—or indeed anything that is thinking of you at all."

Abel did as his father directed and, to his surprise, found that he was once again comfortable. "The cold isn't as cold as I thought it was," he remarked.

Adam shrugged. "The mountain was only heavy because the cockroach tried to hold it on his back."

Adam and his son soon resumed their journey, and, as they were nearing camp, Adam said, "There's almost always a way to move alongside the power of the elements. Never oppose them

directly as though they were enemies to be over-
come. If you do, you'll be crushed like an egg
under a boulder."

GAZELLE
ON A
STRING

The place by the marsh was at the edge of a wide savannah, and one day Adam took his son into the grasses to stalk the gazelles that fed there. For many hours the hunters followed the herd, carefully staying downwind of it. Abel asked his father what they were waiting for, but Adam gave him a signal that said: Be still and watch.

After several more hours had passed, Adam made another sign that said: Be alert now. At that moment, a lion bounded out of the grass and into the midst of the gazelles, bringing one down quickly while the rest fled in all directions.

When it was all over, Adam asked Abel what he had seen. "The lion killed a gazelle," the boy said.

"Yes," Adam replied. "But we're not here to study the

lion, since it's not our prey. It's the gazelles we're interested in. What did you learn about them?" Abel considered this for a time, but beyond the fact that they had fled when the lion appeared, he could think of nothing to say.

"You were absorbed in the spectacle of the kill," Adam said. "But once the lion made its appearance, the kill was all but inevitable and of no interest. You should have been watching and thinking about the rest of the herd. First and most obvious, they abandoned their fallen companion without a moment's hesitation." Abel protested that this was how all herd animals behave.

"That's not so," Adam replied. "A band of baboons might well have turned on the lion and torn it to shreds. However, that's not the important point. Come on, let's see if we can find where the gazelles have reassembled."

When they had once again located the grazing herd, Adam signaled to his son to watch the gazelles, not him. Adam then rose up out of the grass and with a roar plunged into the middle of the startled herd. Suddenly the air was filled with gazelles bounding off in all directions. But Abel was surprised to see that their flight ended as quickly as it had begun. Within moments the gazelles were calmly grazing again as if nothing had happened.

"The gazelles don't have to run to the ends of the earth to escape a lion," his father explained. "A single burst of speed will carry them beyond pursuit whether the lion makes its kill or not. If the lion makes its kill, further pursuit is unnecessary, and if it misses its kill, further pursuit is pointless, because the lion has no hope of outmatching the gazelles' speed once they're alerted. Either way, a single bound is as good as a thousand once the gazelles have evaded the lion's first blow."

"But if the lion misses its kill, won't it stalk the gazelles one by one?" Abel asked.

"It may," Adam replied. "But what of it? Do you think the gazelles should run to the ends of the earth every time a lion is in the neighborhood? What would they find there except another lion? There's no point in running to the ends of the earth when a single burst of speed will put you out of reach of any predator."

Abel thought about this for a while, then shook his head. "I understand what you've said, but I don't see how it helps us, since we're not lions."

"It helps because we're not lions."

But Abel just shook his head again.

"Look," Adam said, "the gazelles' flight is designed to protect it from the lion, which will ordinarily not trouble itself to stalk its prey one by one. It prefers to attack the herd, where its chances of success are greater.

"But we're not lions, and the gazelles' burst of speed can't defeat our greater cunning and patience. Watch me now, but stay well behind."

Adam began to stalk one of the gazelles from the still scattered herd. As he approached it from the rear, the gazelle raised its head and looked uneasily from side to side, and Adam froze in midstep until the gazelle began grazing again. When Adam was some twenty paces away, the gazelle again looked up, and Adam again froze in his tracks. The gazelle studied the man for some moments and then, seeing no harm in him, peacefully returned to its feeding. But when Adam was ten paces away, the gazelle, perhaps disturbed by some noise, trotted off uncertainly to a distance of about thirty paces.

Adam circled to get behind the gazelle and once more began to stalk it, pausing whenever it raised its head. In a few minutes he was close enough to reach out and touch it. He laid his hand gently on its rump and spoke a few words, and the startled gazelle bounded out of sight.

"Now you try it," Adam told his son. "And remember this: When the gazelle looks up, you're not a hunter but a tree."

Abel then selected a gazelle and began to stalk it, but with little of his father's skill. Again and again he signaled his approach when he was still fifty paces away, and the gazelle moved off uneasily. Adam saw that Abel was gradually herding the gazelle into the marshland near their camp, where it would be even more nervous than before. Still he said nothing and dropped farther and farther behind until the

boy was out of sight. He then cut a long strip of bark from a tree and settled down to fashion a length of twine from the fiber on its underside.

Before long Abel returned, and Adam could see from his face that he hadn't been successful in stalking his gazelle.

"What you need," Adam said, "is to have a bit of twine around the gazelle's neck. Then it will be yours."

Abel laughed ruefully and asked how he was supposed to get near enough to the gazelle to loop a bit of twine around its neck.

"That's not what I mean," Adam said. "Here, I'll show you." Adam tied one end of the cord around his waist and handed the other to his son. "I'm the gazelle, you're the stalker. The cord is what binds us together. Now I'm going off to graze, and every time I become aware that you're holding the other end of the cord, I'll let you know."

Adam then moved off, and when he reached the end of the cord he felt a tug at his waist. He looked around suspiciously, and said to Abel, "Who are you and why are you stalking me?"

"I'm a hunter," Abel replied.

Adam laughed. "You're supposed to be a tree, not a hunter. And don't look me in the eye when I turn around."

Adam then moved off again but immediately felt a tug at his waist. He stopped and looked around suspiciously, but Abel was doing his best to look like a tree. "That's better," Adam said. "But you must be ready to move when I move or I'll feel your hand at the other end of the cord every time."

Once again Adam moved off. For a few moments the tension on the cord was steady and slight, but then he felt it go slack at his waist. "What's this? Someone must be creeping up on me!"

He turned and saw that Abel was indeed a pace closer than before.

"You have to keep a steady tension on the cord, Abel. Otherwise you won't know what I'm going to do at any moment—though I'll know what you're doing. If the cord goes slack, I know you must be gaining on me."

Adam moved off again and this time felt no tug or slackening at his waist. "Good," he said as he continued to walk forward. "Now we're bound together, hunter and hunted. But the cord that binds us together is not just the thing in your hand. Let your eyes and ears and skin be the cord as well, and let it tell you my thoughts. Let it tell you when I'm going to pause to browse, when I'm going to move away again, and when I catch sight of a succulent clump of grass to one side or another."

Soon Abel was following his father's movements smoothly and easily without signaling his presence, and Adam said, "Now, very patiently, you can begin working yourself closer to me. Remember that, because your cord is around me, I'm already yours. You need only draw me in like a fish, hand over hand. But be careful not to change the tension on the cord."

And before long Abel was close enough to reach out and touch his father's shoulder.

By now it was nearly dark, and Adam and his son turned back toward their camp. For a while they walked in silence, then Abel said, "Still, I'm not sure what I've learned. I know the feeling in the cord around your waist and could follow you easily now. But I'll never have a cord around a gazelle's neck to follow."

"You will if the gazelle belongs to you," Adam replied. "Your path and the gazelle's are part of a web endlessly woven in the hands of the god. If the gazelle is yours, you and it will be tied together as surely as you and I were. But I can't tell you how to find that thread. You'll know it when it's in your hands."

FINDING AN ACCOMMODATION WITH THE SEA

Once, when Adam and his family were camped by the river that flows into the sea, Adam let his son lead in tracking a boar. When the track disappeared into thick underbrush, Abel circled the thicket only to find that it fronted the river, which the boar had evidently crossed. Abel led his father across the river, where he hoped to pick up the boar's trail again. But the shores of the river were rocky, and Abel could find no trace of the boar's passing.

Adam sat down with his back against a tree while Abel dashed up and down the water's edge and poked here and there along the inland trails. An endless line of ants were marching past Adam's tree, and, as he waited for his son to pick up the boar's trail, he amused himself by watching them making their way in the dust.

Abel, angry and frustrated by his failure to find the lost trail, soon came over to where his father was sitting and glared down at him impatiently. Adam, paying his son no attention, laid a leaf in the way of the ants and, when a few had clambered up onto it, set it to one side of their path. The ants swarmed off the leaf in

confusion and began circling in all directions in a frantic effort to find their mysteriously missing companions.

Abel could contain his impatience no longer, and he said, "Why are you playing with these stupid ants when our boar is getting farther and farther away?"

Adam laughed and said, "These stupid ants were trying to teach you the proper way to find a lost trail. But since you were too furious to watch, you missed the whole thing and the ants are already back in line. Watch, and I'll show you again."

This time Adam picked up a single ant and set it to one side of the trail.

As Abel watched, he realized that the movements which a moment before had seemed frantic and random were in fact full of purpose and method. The ant walked for a bit in a straight line, paused, then swung in an arc back to its point of departure, where it hesitated again before extending the line in the other direction and making a still wider arc back to the other side of the line. In this way, its circle of search grew steadily, arc after arc, until it intersected the line of marching ants. Then the lost worker resumed its place in line without missing a step.

"Make the river the baseline of your search," Adam told his son. "Start with a small arc from upriver to downriver. When you come back to the river, take another step upriver, then circle back downriver. Eventually your trail and the boar's will have to cross."

Following the example of the ants, Abel soon raised the boar's trail, and the two hunters were on their way again. The trail led steadily on toward the sea and clearer ground, so that Adam and Abel quickly made up the time they'd lost and were not far behind the boar. After making sure of their weapons, they hurried on. But before they had a chance to use them, they found themselves standing on the shore of the sea, where, to their surprise, they saw their quarry swimming placidly away.

"Now that's a thing I've never seen," Adam said, but Abel asked, "Aren't we going in after it?"

Adam shook his head. "You'll never catch it in the water," he said. "And what would you do with it if you did?" But Abel was determined to have the boar he'd tracked for so many hours and he rushed into the sea.

Adam smiled and sat down on the shore to wait. Before long, however, he heard his son crying for help a hundred yards from shore. Looking out to sea, Adam saw Abel standing in water no higher than his chest.

"What's the matter?" Adam shouted.

"I can't move!" Abel shouted back. "The water is dragging me out to sea!"

As Adam waded out to where his son was standing, he felt the growing pressure of an undertow clutch his legs. Coming abreast of Abel, he said, "Well, now we're both here in the grip of the elements. Shall we struggle and drown or stand here and starve to death?"

"I didn't know what to do," Abel replied. "I felt that if I let go, I would be swept out to sea."

"And so you would have been," Adam replied. "I've told you that there's almost always a way to flow alongside the elements. But that doesn't mean turning your life over to them like a leaf in the wind. It doesn't mean collapsing helplessly and letting the elements do what they will with you."

Then Adam asked, "Where is it you want to go?"

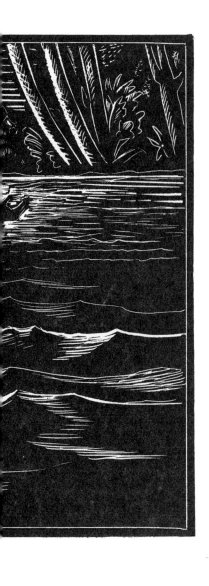

"Toward shore," Abel replied.

"And have you tried to go toward shore? Show me."

Abel leaned into the water but he said, "I'm afraid to lift my feet. If I lose my footing, I'll be swept away."

Adam nodded thoughtfully. "You're doing exactly what I told you not to do. You're opposing this flow of water directly; you're assaulting it like an enemy. Earlier today, when the boar's tracks disappeared into a thicket, you didn't oppose that obstacle directly. You didn't plunge into the thicket; you went around it, knowing that it's senseless to assault an impassable spot just because it happens to be in front of you. There was bound to be a passable spot to one side or the other, and you went looking for it. Use the same sense here that you used when you faced the thicket."

After a few moments of thought, Abel began walking along parallel to the shore, and Adam followed. After a few hundred yards they found a place where the pull of the undertow began to slacken, and little by little they made their way back to dry land.

As they turned toward camp, Abel asked his father if he thought the boar had been carried out to sea.

"Possibly," Adam replied. "But not for the reason you might have been. It would never occur to the boar to oppose the undertow directly, because it would never occur to it that the undertow was an enemy bent on its destruction. It would try to go around it like any other obstacle. All the same, it may have been carried out to sea."

Later Adam said, "Sometimes there's no way to move alongside the elements and survive, or the way may be blocked. Then it's time to open yourself to death in the same way you opened yourself to the cold in the little hills. After that, if you survive, you will never again have to be afraid of death, just as now you never will again have to be afraid of the cold."

THE WEB
WOVEN
ENDLESSLY

When it was near the time for Abel to become a man, Adam said to him: "You know that I've taught you many things: to give a stone a cutting edge, to set a spear point solidly, to lay a cunning snare, to make a warm tent, to spin strong twine from bark, and so on. The results of these activities are all useful, but they are also all destined for the trash heap in the end. The dust beneath our feet is full of the discarded products of such ingenuity.

"My gift to you is not the knowledge of making useful trash, for one may live well without such knowledge. But there is other knowledge without which no one can live well, and this is my gift to you. The name of this knowledge is wisdom. It is the gift my father gave to me and his father gave to him. Remember it for yourself and for your children."

Then Adam said: "The first gift of wisdom is the gift of seeing beneath the surface of things and calling them by their true names. Until now you have named things as they have seemed, not knowing that they have other names that come nearer the truth. This is because children see only the surface of things. When you come to a land where the people marvel at the wisdom of their children, know that you are in a land of fools.

"The child looks at you, at me, at your mother and calls us men and women. But the child sees only our appearance, for we are not men and women, we are deer. The flesh that grows upon our bones is the flesh of deer, for it is made from the flesh of deer we have eaten. The eyes that move in our heads are the eyes of deer, and we look at the world in their stead and see what they might have seen. The fire of life that once burned in the deer now burns in us, and we live their lives and walk in their tracks across the hand of god.

"The child looks at the sea that rolls endlessly across the plains and calls it grass. But this is not grass. This is deer and bison and sheep and cicadas and moles and rabbits. This handful of stalks here—this is a mouse. And the mouse, the ox, the gazelle, the goat, and the beetle all burn with the fire of grass. Grass is their mother and father, and their young are grass.

"The child sees a swarm of creatures dancing across the plain and calls them grasshoppers. But he's only looking at their horny shells. They're not grasshoppers. They're sparrows, and soon their armor will be transformed into feathers and they'll take their dance into the sky.

"One thing: grass and grasshopper. One thing: grasshopper and sparrow. One thing: sparrow and fox. One thing: fox and vulture. One thing, and its name is fire, burning today as a stalk in the field, tomorrow as a rabbit in its burrow, and the next day as a man in his tent.

"The vulture is fox; the fox, grasshopper; the

grasshopper, rabbit; the rabbit, man; the man, grass. All together, we are the life of this place, indistinguishable from one another, intermingling in the flow of fire, and the fire is god.

"To each is given its moment in the blaze, its spark to be surrendered to another when it is sent, so that the blaze may go on. None may deny its spark to the general blaze and live forever. Each is sent to another someday. You are sent; you are on your way. I am sent. To the wolf or the lion or the vulture or the grasses, I am sent.

"My death is the life of another, and I will stand again in the windswept grasses and look through the eyes of the fox and take the air with the eagle and run in the track of the deer."

For a time Adam was silent. Then he went on: "The second gift of wisdom is the gift of tracking, of discerning the true course of things.

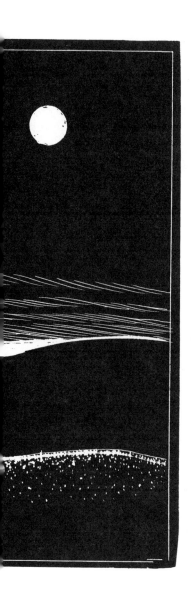

As my father showed them to me, I show you now the tracks of everything.

"Remember the place by the rock, the place under the little hills, the place in the marsh, the place in the desert, and the place by the river that runs into the sea. These in their order and season are our tracks through time, land-marks found for our journey across the hand of god. This journey embeds us in the cycle of life, in the fire that burns forever. In it, we find our place. In it, we live. A tent is not our shelter. Rather, the journey is our shelter.

The journey is the song we make of our lives. We're not crafters of axes or spears or tents or baskets. These are trifles. We are seekers of holy places.

"We make our journey in the company of others; the deer, the rabbit, the bison, and the quail walk before us, and the lion, the eagle, the wolf, the vulture, and the hyena walk behind us. All our paths lie together in the hand of god and none is wider than any other or favored above any other. The worm that creeps beneath your foot is making its journey across the hand of god as surely as you are.

"Wherever life moves, the hand of god is under it, so no step can be off the path. When you stumble on the mountainside, that is part of your path. When your child is sick and you turn aside from the hunt, that is part of your path. When you wander hungry in the desert and cannot find your way, you're not lost, you're on your path. When cunning fails and your prey eludes you, don't curse your luck; this fruitless hunt is part of your path.

"Many paths end at the point of your spear or on the edge of your harvesting knife. What you take, take compassionately, saying, 'You are sent to me by the god. I take you for my need.' Remember that when hunter and prey meet, both are standing in their tracks. You are sent to the deer no less than the deer is sent to you, and the god means the deer to have your gift as surely as it means you to have the deer's.

"We share this world with others who are not beasts or men or the spirits of men or gods. They are denizens of wastelands and barrens, of deserts and high places where nothing grows, and they don't follow the deer or the quail, nor are they followed by the lion or the hyena. All the same, they're making their journey in the hand of the god just as we are. What destiny they pursue in their journey I cannot say, for their tracks run beyond ours and where they end no man will ever know. Nevertheless all journeys are in the hand of god, and it may be that theirs and ours are being woven together even now. For from each generation a few of us are called to track them to their haunts and, through contending with them, to win their alliance and their guidance to power and wisdom beyond the common run. If you're ever prompted to search them out, arm yourself with courage and discretion, as you would for a battle for your life. They're not to be trifled with.

"Remember that your tracks are one strand of the web woven endlessly in the hand of god. They're tied to those of the mouse in the field, the eagle on the mountain, the crab in its hold, the lizard beneath its rock. The leaf that falls to the ground a thousand miles away touches your life. The impress of your foot in the soil is felt through a thousand generations.

"Remember too that the person standing in your tracks is you. Never say, like a child, 'My brother made me do this' or 'My wife made me do this' or 'The gods made me do this.' The tracks you make are your own. Stand in them bravely."

Next Adam said: "The third gift of wisdom is the gift of reading the message of events. When the gods made the universe, they made it in such a way that all who have eyes to see can read the Law of Life in it. They wrote it in things, not in words, so that not only man but the snail and the mosquito and the rabbit could read it.

"This is why no man will ever succeed in framing the Law in words: it is too simple for

•

words. Should you meet some skeptic who says to you, 'Where is this Law? I see no Law,' tell him to watch the wolf and the deer and the jackal and live as they do. These creatures see the Law and are following it, and there are no criminals among them.

"From time to time some creature will go mad and break the Law of Life. This happens among beasts and men as well. Their dreams are incomprehensible; they imagine that the spark of life in them belongs to them forever and need not be returned to the general blaze.

"When this happens to a man, he's capable of anything. He'll stir up trouble among his companions, assault them, even murder them. In time of need, he'll refuse to share what he has. He'll say, 'This is my spear, don't touch it; if you die for lack of a spear, then die.' A man like this must be stopped, but not with cruelty;

with pity, for he has somehow been injured in spirit and has gone mad. The Law of Life will tell you how this is to be done. If there's nowhere to put your sleeping mat except on the place where the thornbush grows, you pluck it out, saying, 'I pluck you out of need, because I am only a man and must sleep in order to live.' If there's nowhere to put your camp except by the rock where the viper lives, you drive the viper away. But if it will not be driven away, then you kill it, saying, 'I kill you out of need, because I am only a man and must move around my camp without having to watch out for vipers.'

"If it comes to this, you must deal with troublemakers in the same way, because you are only men and women and must live in harmony among yourselves. At first, make fun of the troublemaker and let him see with good humor that his behavior makes him a fool. If he reforms, cease your joking and never refer to his misbehavior again. But if he doesn't reform, draw away from him until he has no one to talk to, no one to hunt with, no one to help him if he's sick or injured. If he then comes to you and says, 'I made a good kill today, let's share it,' you'll know he wants to reform. Receive him back into the community without a word of reproach and let him mend his ways. But if he doesn't reform and continues to make trouble for those around him, drive him away and post a guard to see that he doesn't return. If, after a time, he asks to be allowed to join the circle around the fire once again or somehow demonstrates his willingness to reform, receive him back into the community without a word of reproach and treat him as you did before he became a troublemaker. But if he still doesn't reform and refuses to be driven away and continues to assault the harmony of the community, then, if all agree, he must be killed. This should be done by his own family, if possible; then there will be no reproach for the rest of the community later on. Let him be killed in his sleep, if possible, and mercifully, saying, 'We kill you out of need, because we are only humans and must live as humans without cowering before the madness that afflicts you."

Then Adam went on in the same vein: "God writes not only in things but in events, and to read this writing is the subtlest wisdom of all.

"You need not be afraid of pitting your strength against anything, but a wise man doesn't throw himself against the flowing tide, saying, 'I will overpower it.' But neither does he let the tide sweep him away, saying, 'Oh, the gods want my life now!' Instead he moves across the flow and finds the channel of retreat that the gods have left for him.

"Here's a story for you about this: One day a man was out hunting and saw a ram on the hillside. He said to himself, 'I don't know whether this ram is mine or whether it has some business to finish, but there's only one way to find out.' And he pursued the ram with all his strength. But before long, he stumbled on a stone and fell down. He picked himself up, saying, 'Well, it may be that the gods have other plans for this ram, but there's still only one way to find out,' and he hurried on. But before long, he slipped on a root and fell into a gully. Without pausing to count his bruises, he picked himself up again, saying, 'Perhaps that ram has another day to live. Nevertheless, there's still only one way to find out,' and he continued the chase like a true hunter. But before long, he dislodged a stone and started a landslide that carried him halfway down the hill, covering him with bumps and bruises. Still, he picked himself up and started off again, saying, 'This may be my day to go hungry, but, in spite of everything, there's only one way to find out.'

"Now as it happens, the ram did indeed have some business to finish, and the gods had not meant it for the man. But seeing how determined the hunter was, the gods said to themselves, 'It seems that this man's need is greater than the ram's business, so let's give it to him.' And before long, without any more mishaps, the hunter closed with his quarry and killed it. 'At last I know!' the hunter said to himself then. 'This ram was mine in spite of everything.' And of course he was right.

"Now here's a second story about this. It's

about the same hunter and it goes along in the same way up to the point of the landslide. As before, the ram did have some business to finish and the gods had not meant it for the man. But, in spite of the man's determination, the gods knew that the ram's business was greater than the man's need, and they could not let him have it. So they said to themselves, 'The hunter must be stopped from killing this ram.' And sure enough, a little while later the hunter fell into a crevice and twisted his ankle so that he could hardly walk. 'At last I know!' the hunter cried then. 'This ram had some business to finish and he wasn't mine.' And of course he was right.

"Now here's a third story about this. It's about the same hunter and it goes along in the same way up to the point of the man's falling into the crevice and twisting his ankle. Instead of accepting the fact that the ram was not his, the hunter pulled himself up and limped ahead in terrible pain, saying, 'In spite of everything, there's still only one way to find out!'

"Now the gods were baffled at this man's folly and wondered what they could do to stop him. 'It would seem,' they said to themselves, 'that nothing less than toppling the mountain over on him will make him abandon his hunt.' And sure enough, before long, the mountain toppled over on the man, and just before he was crushed under it, he said, 'At last I know!' And that was the end of him.

"These three stories were given to me by my father, and I don't know any better way to tell you about this than to repeat them. When you act, act wholeheartedly and with an undivided will, but leave your ears open to the message of events and don't force the gods to topple mountains onto you before you understand."

Then Adam said, "Now here's another story for you in the same vein. It happened once that a band of lions and a band of wolves lived in adjoining territories, and each was an annoyance to the other, for one time the wolves would hunt in the lions' territory and another time the lions would hunt in the wolves' territory. So the lions finally said to themselves, 'Let's put an end to this rivalry once and for all. Tonight, near dawn, let's fall upon the wolves and destroy them down to the last cub.' And that's exactly what they did.

"Thereafter the lions had an easy time of it indeed. Since they didn't have to share it with the wolves, the game became so plentiful that they hardly had to do more than step outside their den to capture a meal. They had many cubs, who grew up well fed and playful. But one old lion looked at what was happening and said, 'I think we've made a mistake. Our cubs are growing up fat and slow and placid. This is not the way lions should be. They should be lean and fast and fierce, as we were when we were young.'

"The other lions laughed at him and said, 'How can our cubs be lean when there's so much game? Why should they be fast when they need only reach out a paw to have a meal? And why should they be fierce when our enemies have all been destroyed?'

"So the old lion was silenced, and the cubs grew to maturity as fat and slow and good-natured as puppies. But one day a pack of wild dogs appeared from the north, driven from their territory by drought. They were lean and hungry and fast and fierce, and when the lions objected to their encroachment, the dogs fell upon the lions and easily tore them to shreds.

"So you see that the old lion was right. Although the lions were not wise enough to see it, their ancient rivals, the wolves, and been keeping them alive, and when they destroyed the wolves they destroyed themselves as well. Even if the pack of dogs hadn't come along, the first drought or flood to come along would have finished them off as easily. But of course this is only a story. Lions know the Law of Life and follow it and would never behave so foolishly.

"Like the lions, men are predators, and like all predators, we get tired of competing with others for game. But however tired we become of them, these competitors are needful to our life, for without them we'd grow fat and slow and placid, and sooner or later we'd perish. All this is true of our human rivals as well. From time to time we show our neighbors that we haven't grown fat and placid—and they do the same for us!

"When the need arises, be fierce and resolute in battle, but remember that these rivals are sent to you for your life as surely as the deer. Respect them as you respect the deer and be generous to the wives and children of those you slay in battle; a warrior who is both valiant and great-hearted will be sung for many generations."

Then Adam said in the same vein:

"Just as no amount of effort will block the tide, no amount of effort will bring an event to fruition before its time. A man cannot learn to be a hunter before he becomes a hunter. Hunting simply cannot be learned in advance of hunting. It's the same with becoming an adult. A child can no more learn to be an adult before he's an adult than a man can learn to be a hunter before he hunts. This is why everything is permitted to you today, because you're still a child. But tomorrow, when you're a man, the things permitted to you as a child will be permitted to you no longer. If today you smash your spear against a rock in a fit of temper, I will laugh and make you a new one, because today you're still a child. But if you do the same tomorrow you'll make a new spear for yourself or go hungry, because tomorrow you'll be a man, even as I am, and must begin to be responsible for your life.

"This is the meaning of the rites of initiation into adulthood: not that you have learned to be an adult, but that you must begin to learn. The day after your initiation, your thoughts will be the same as those of the day before, but you will nevertheless be accorded the rights of an adult and be expected to fulfill the obligations of an adult. And you will learn to cope with both in the same way you learned to be a hunter: by beginning."

At last Adam said: "You're beginning to know the Law of Life. I too am beginning to know the Law of Life. If you ask me on my last day, as I close my eyes for the last time, whether I know the Law of Life, I'll tell you: 'I'm beginning to know it.'

"If any man tells you he knows the whole of the Law of Life or that he can encompass it in words, that man is a fool or a liar, because the Law of Life is written in the universe and no man can know the whole of it. If ever you're in doubt about the Law, consult the caterpillar or the gull or the jackal; no man will ever know it better or follow it more steadfastly than they."

Then, in concluding, Adam said: "Wisdom is the gift I give to you, nothing else. This is my legacy to you, the legacy I received from my father and he received from his father. It is the legacy of generations, from one to the next for all time. Your tools will grow blunt, your spears will shatter, your tents will crumble, your twine will fray, but this knowledge I've given you will not wear out. In a thousand generations it will still be as strong as it was a thousand generations ago."